"The voyeuristic and sadomasochistic latency in art and sex is on stark display in Boston-Manzetti's epic, with its cinematic images giving flesh to daemonic street theater where anything can be sacrificed.

"With startlingly economical poetry, the authors give gritty vitality to the lowlife souls whose moment-to-moment movements are subconscious rituals of destruction.

"*Sacrificial Nights* hits just the right notes—with the heavy blow of a Death Metal sledgehammer or the soft whisper of an Xacto blade through flesh."

—Randy Chandler,
coauthor with t. winter-damon of *Duet for the Devil* and *Forbidden Gospels: The Devil's Cut*

Sacrificial Nights

Bruce Boston

Alessandro Manzetti

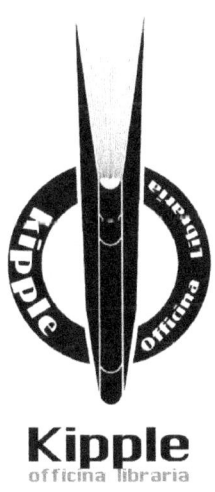

Kipple
officina libraria

"Jean-Paul, the Flying Thief" appeared in *Illumen*, fall, 2015. "Lady of the Dark Hours" appeared in *Devolution Z*, December, 2015. "The Great Unknown" appeared in *Illumen*, spring, 2016. "Legend of the Albino Snakes and the Bloody Child" appeared in Polu Texni, April, 2016. All other poems appear here for the first time.

] FUORI [
[COLLANA]

Fuori (collana) (serie) 12
ISBN 978-88-98953-55-4

I Edition - June, 2016
Copyright (edition) © 2016 Kipple Officina Libraria
Cover Art and illustrations © 2016 Ben Baldwin

Kipple Officina Libraria
Via Ignazio Canale 5/2
16029 Torriglia (GE) ITALY
www.kipple.it

CONTENTS

9   Route 66

10   Slade, Mary Ann, and Pet

14   Jean-Paul, the Flying Thief

20   Gasoline

23   Sandoval and the Night Creatures

26   Eugene, Arsonist

30   Sandoval's Nightmare Sampler

33   Fade Away

37   Rose and the White Stalker

42   Cannibal at Large

45   Eugene's Hurt

50   Requiem in a Taxi

52   The Xacto Killer: Interior Monologue

55   Deep in His Coma

60   Rose's Trauma

64   Eugene Hates the Rain

67   Awakening

74   Lady of the Dark Hours

77   Betrayed by the Rain

80   Obsessed with Autumn

83   Sandoval Bitters: Interior Monologue

86   Death Metal in a Taxi/Strawberry Fields in a Car

91   The Great Unknown

99   I Am the Fire

103   Conflagration

121   Legend of the Albino Pythons and the Bloody Child

Illustrations 13, 22, 46, 66, 94, 102. 124

Contributors 127

Bruce Boston – Alessandro Manzetti

Sacrificial Nights

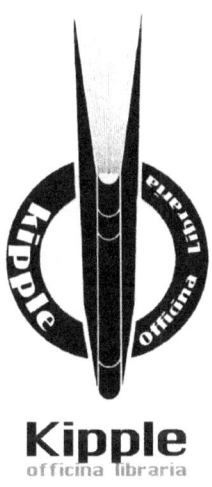

Kipple
officina libraria

Sacrificial Nights
is a poetry novella,
and was written to
be read sequentially

ROUTE 66
Boston-Manzetti

See that guy over in the corner.
the one with long hair and a beard,
nursing a Budweiser and scribbling
in a spiral-bound notebook.
Claims he's a poet.
Calls himself "Route 66."
"It's all about escape," he says.

Sometimes he tells us tales,
his poetry, I guess it is,
of a city where he once lived,
a sacrificial city , or so he claims.

Don't know much about poetry
but we always listen,
cause he takes us to another world.

SLADE, MARY ANN & PET
Boston-Manzetti

The python twists her thick
diamond-backed hide
down the dingy third floor
of a decrepit brownstone.
This is her hunting ground.
The rattletrap cage elevator,
a thornless iron maiden,
groans and creaks upward.
The python is deaf as all
of her kind, but she can feel
the vibrations growing stronger.
Could be prey approaching.
She slithers into the shadows.

"Third door on the right,"
Slade had told the john
as he pocketed the man's cash.
"You'll get the ride of your life!"
The man emerges from the
cage of the elevator and
is drawn down the corridor,
littered with assorted trash.

He is feeling a bit trapped
between old posters of Gauguin,
between too many washed-out
slices of a deformed Tahiti

resembling some surreal
hell in the abridged light.

Third door on the right is ajar.
The man catches his breath
as he enters and sees her
lying naked on the bed,
a light-skinned black girl,
just the way he likes them.

He is stunned by the scents
of mango and pomegranate
with which Mary Ann has
anointed her young body,
both laced with soporifics
to which she has long
since grown immune.

The python follows the client
with her ancient reptilian radar.
She sniffs his trail of loneliness
and desire along with the
smells of other men who have
passed down this dim hallway,
Her black tongue flickers
as she slips under the bed,
rolls up all of her length,
and waits patiently for Mary
to finish her ministrations.
She dreams of the rainforest,

the taste of monkeys and
coatimundi and rats,
the rough bark of trees
against her sleek skin,
all the stuff of her past.

Down in the street, leaning
back on the leather upholstery
of his dark blue Mercedes,
— no flash and bling for one
who always plays it cool —
Slade puffs idly on a reefer
rolled in liquorice paper
by one of his favourite girls.

He knows full well why
some of his customers
never return after having
a session with Mary Ann.
Slade is a tolerant man.
He understands that
certain people have urges
that must be satisfied
— like Mary Ann, like
himself for that matter —
and he admires those who
have learned to sate them.

JEAN-PAUL, THE FLYING THIEF
Boston-Manzetti

Summer.

The apartment is dark.

A small circle of light
runs up the ivory wallpaper,
penetrates a fissure
of the Boulle furniture,
awakens the woodworms,
asleep in their gnawed galleries.
This alien sun is the torch
of the thief Jean-Paul.

He is doing his job,
the only job he knows,
sweating and cursing,
followed by a train of moths
that appeared from nowhere,
drawn by the light.
"Damned beasts!"

Jean-Paul hears a noise.
Something is moving
in the next room.
The cocaine in his veins
melds with an adrenaline rush.
He releases the safety
on his revolver.
"Bloody hell."

The light of the torch enters
the room and is drawn
to the ornate chandelier,
its crystals crashing into pieces
before Jean-Paul's stoned eyes,
a thousand slanting rays.

His vision clicks
like a lantern show
of dislocated time
from one image to the next.

He sees himself climbing
the rickety fire escape,
sees himself as if
he were a being floating
in the air beyond.

Sees himself
prying the window open
and climbing awkwardly
into the room.

Sees himself as a patient
etherized upon a table,
the worn and worried eyes
of half-masked faces
looming above him.

Jean-Paul shakes his

head and looks down,
blinking from the reflections.
There is no one here:
no men, ghosts or cops.

A blue-skinned painting,
a stormy sea in the manner of Turner,
shifts inexplicably back and forth,
rubbing against one wall.
"Here's the noise. Son of a bitch!"
There is no danger, perhaps.

The moths multiply,
continue to fly in a circle
around the head of the thief,
as if he were the only lighthouse
in thousands of miles of darkness.

Jean-Paul takes off his cap
and swipes them away.
"It's hot in here, too damn hot!"

Yet all at once his skin feels refreshed.
The tongue of a subtle wind
is licking his cheeks and forehead,
even though the windows are shut.

The sails of the Turner ship
billow and swell to bursting,
and Jean-Paul can hear

the shouts of the sailors,
curses and cries of despair
swallowed by the storm.
He can smell the brine
of the crashing waves.

He is enveloped by a vision
of his mother and father,
his older brother,
all dead and buried,
riding the wings of that storm,
arms outstretched, legs straight,
their faces drawn back,
as if they had been
crucified upon the wind.

The thief begins
to distrust his mind,
the stuff that he bought
in the parking lot
before going to work.

That dealer, Josh,
strange guy,
looked more like an insect
than a human being,
scrawny, with those thin ears
laid back against his skull,
his arms held out

and bent at the elbows
like some praying mantis,
and dark impenetrable eyes,
just like the eyes
of those damned moths
now covering Jean-Paul
in a fluttering coat
like a second skin.

He drops the torch
and it flickers into darkness.
Like the moths, he is
now drawn to the only
visible light in the room,
the lamppost beyond the
window in the street below.

The moths begin batting
against the window
and Jean-Paul has
become one of them,
batting against the window,
trying to get to the light.

The glass shatters outward
in a starburst rush
and he is flying
like a magical being,
his features taut,
his hair blown back,

until he sees the asphalt
rushing up to greet him.

Deep in his coma,
Jean-Paul dreams he is a moth,
dreams he is a thief who can fly,
dreams of a thousand unlocked doors
and open windows.

"Bloody hell."

GASOLINE
Manzetti

On the western border of the city,
where Spanish Town sprawls
into the adjacent suburbs,
Camilla sits at her favorite table
in the bar of the *Gracias Madre*.
While outside on the street
they sell plastic Christmas trees,
hot pastries, fake passports,
candies filled with paradise juice.

On the old jukebox in the corner
Chavela Vargas is singing *"La Llorona."*
The guitar strings count the notes
like fingers on the beads of a rosary.
The green curtains on the window,
dotted with small white flowers,
look destined to live forever
without losing their colors,
like the world behind the shoulders
of Frida Kahlo on her iconic *Vogue* cover.
Camilla is staring at her chip engagement ring.
It's so tight she can't pull it off.

A brand new Ford pick-up filled
with melancholy workers of the night,
a Christ sticker glued to the license plate,
stops in front of the windows of the bar.

In the driver's seat, a young bastard
with too many possible fathers,
doomed by the sombrero
he imagines atop his head.

A man with an unstitched soul
and an atlas of hell on his scarred face
sucks the finger of Camilla until the ring slips off.
He downs the last shot of Bushmills.
"We can call him Diego," he says
though he will remain only in your head."
The wet poison on her finger
dries under the fan blades.

The time has come again.
She must don her high heel shoes,
empty and asleep under the table,
and go back to work once more.
All the hookers call that man Gasoline
because he makes your belly burn
like boiling tequila,
like a ceaseless miscarriage.

SANDOVAL AND THE NIGHT CREATURES
Boston

Pimps, whores, pickpockets,
drunks, drug addicts, dealers,
psychotics, peeping toms,
burglars, ethnic gangs,
serial rapists and serial killers,
all creatures of the night,
all creatures of the city,
all creatures that gave
Detective Samuel Sandoval
a fierce and pounding headache
at one time or another.

Sandoval would take two aspirin,
and when that only dulled
the pain a bit, two more
with a glass of milk,
so they wouldn't ravage
his stomach lining completely.

Sandoval was a family man
with a wife and two children,
a normal man by his own estimation.
He lived in a modest suburb
18.7 miles from city limits,
21 miles from the inner-city hellhole
where he worked the night shift.

Sometimes he thought

that Fate had chosen him
in its perverse way
because he hated the night
more than any other officer,
because he despised the misfits
who inhabited it and ran riot
through its darkened streets.
There were times he wanted
to kill every last one of them.

Sandoval would stumble home
from a night of headaches,
his temples still throbbing
in the early morning hours,
to endure a troubled sleep
well into the afternoon.

Sometimes he would awaken
from a forgotten nightmare,
drenched in a cold sweat,
an incomplete cry upon his lips,
the remnants of terrifying images
swirling through his head.

He would awaken lost
and alone in a king-sized bed,
his wife Janine out shopping
or ferrying the kids somewhere,
yet never there by his side
to hold and comfort him.

And Sandoval's greatest fear,
recalled in fragments
from more than a few
of his daytime nightmares,
was not that he would
be killed or disabled
by some chance encounter
with a gang member,
not that he would
break down completely
from the endless strain,
but that through some
rogue twist of Fate
he would be transformed
from a respected officer
into a creature of the night,
lost beyond redemption,
no better than any of them.

EUGENE, ARSONIST
Manzetti

Eugene "Two Hearts" has been freed from the asylum.
His jaws are clicking, they seem to chew the air,
the fresh, tasty freedom of the night
lying in front of him with its legs open.
He wants to have sex immediately,
to forget the invisible butterflies,
the bars of steel, the blue and red pills,
the three years passed in his cell
between the padded walls of his blind Nirvana.
Even a ghost, a murderer such as he,
has the right to fuck.

He's holding a piece of paper.
On it is the address of the Eldorado,
a brothel that sits atop a dim bistro
that swallows the dark coats and sluts
of greedy rich people who like to slum.
The pair stand beside a sluggish river
polluted by debris and thick with rats.

Eugene climbs the stairs,
stops for a moment,
looking for something in his pockets.
He pulls out a holy card of Joan of Arc
that burns his fingers,
and a roll of pressed banknotes.
He counts the money, it should be enough

for an hour, perhaps more.
He kisses the armoured mouth of Joan,
makes the sign of the cross and goes on.

Madame Desroches opens the door,
the red jaws of the Eldorado.
She looks at the stubby, old,
deformed shoes of Eugene,
then straightens her big breasts
coming out of the bra,
spits on the ground and croaks:
"Show me your money!"

Eugene is pushed into a living room.
On armchairs covered with heretic lilies
are sitting the wonders of the Eldorado,
waiting for their clients to arrive.
Madame Desroches giggles, coughs.
She knows well that no brothel
in all of the city can compare
with the variety she offers:

Isis with her mouth lapping her ears
in an endless orange smile,
Coralie with her tattooed skin
like a second suit of clothes,
Blanche with three breasts
moving in an impossible dance,
a jelly pantomime.

Dr. Dubois, God of Transformation,
constantly forges new women,
an avant-garde generation of hookers,
daughters of his scalpel and needles.

Eugene "Two Hearts" has no doubts.
He chooses Coralie, who takes him to her room,
another cell, with moths in place of butterflies,
insects and thoughts accustomed to the night,
a row of mirrors reflecting masses of flesh,
chopped fears, marmalade of fleas,
sketches of dreams
on a filthy mattress without sheets.

Coralie takes off her bra
and stretches out on the bed.
She seems a triple Amazon
imprisoned inside a kaleidoscope;
her flesh rotates, multiplying endlessly.
Eugene feels the beating of his left heart,
the one that knows how to love,
the one he thought was broken;
while the other, the right heart
— a freak of nature —
only knows to hate; it loves the fires,
the smell of gasoline and the burning
flesh of women in flames.

That second heart remains silent,
waiting to get the upper hand,

which could be at any moment,
as happened with the last Joan of Arc,
charred to death three years ago.

SANDOVAL'S NIGHTMARE SAMPLER
Boston-Manzetti

Drive That Spike Home

He sits shivering in a shabby room
in a cheap tenement hotel.
His entire body feels sick.
His stomach and heart feel sick,
and there are things crawling under his skin.
He can see them moving
when he looks at his arms and hands,
and his craving is relentless.
All he wants to see is the blood back up the needle
and drive that spike home.
One more fix to get him to morning,
then he goes to rehab.
He swears he will.

Rainbow Snake

Noon, too much light
that reveals bruises, signs
on the body of Cheyenne,
the bitch who doesn't want to open her legs.
Her head is shaved,
she is an unarmed Medusa.
She looks in the mirror, her black tongue licks it,
her breasts are shaking from the pain
and tears are running down her cheeks.
The pimp is engraving her back

with his initials: S.S.
Her flesh burns,
her mouth opens slowly, to whisper,
"I'll birth a rainbow snake
that will never forget your smell"

Black Cab

The arsonist is on the roof.
He observes the burning
while the city sleeps.
The heart of woman is roasting,
her incandescent pearls
accustomed to the ocean
leave her neck, roll away,
fall into the void
like hail from another world.
On the road below,
behind the windshield
of a Black Cab carrying Death
and two cans of gasoline,
Sandoval is the driver.

Aluminum Soul

Sandoval sweats blood
while observing the killer,
who is extracting ruby red
from the womb of the woman.
He can't breathe, can't move,

is bound, hands and feet
by the invisible cables of his dream.
The killer wipes his forehead, smiles,
showing him his two gold incisors.
The blade, with its aluminum soul,
sinks into the flesh of the woman,
cutting tissue and muscles.
White hands search for a black pearl
hidden in the matrix of the woman,
in her screaming abyss.

The red becomes purple,
the deep purple of the bowels,
favorite color of the killer.
It stains his latex gloves,
the old mattress, the hardwood
floor of a building evacuated
and ready to be demolished.

Sandoval hears the noise
beyond the woman's cries,
the howling of bulldozers
that lift their iron tongues
with a roar and thankfully
crush his nightmare.

FADE AWAY
Boston

"Sinners, idolaters, adulterers,
fornicators, prepare yourselves
to roast in the fury and stench
of Satan's caverns evermore!"

He who stands at 5th and Vine
atop an inverted plastic crate
so he might tower a head
above the passing crowds
and chastise them one and all.

He who wears white robes
and crude rope sandals
and carries a hickory staff
he thuds upon the pavement
to emphasize his dire and
indiscriminate accusations.

"Blasphemers! Degenerates!
Reprobates! Hypocrites!"

He who appears on schedule
and without fail to inveigh
against his ever changing
and indifferent flock
as the neon of the night
supersedes the light of day.

He who thunders ominously,
leveling a rigid and gnarled
forefinger at any passing
woman who wears lipstick.

"Scarlet hussy! Temptress!
Your devil charms do not sway
me from the path of the Lord.
Get thee to a nunnery and
repent your wanton ways!"

He who preaches
of a Second Coming,
he who quotes Scripture,
chapter and verse by heart,
he who can rant without
rest for hours on end.

He whose skeletal arms
rise from flapping sleeves,
sweeping this way and that,
lined with dark veins and
protruding tendons like
some detailed map of
the horrors of Gehenna.

"You who will not accept
the Lord into your heart
will never know peace,
will never dwell in

the Kingdom of Heaven."

He whose hair and beard
grow longer and grayer,
whose countenance
darkens and is etched
with lines beneath the
constant neon glare.

He whose once-white robes
grow dirtier through the
passing months and years
until their hemline is
black as the darkest sin.

"If you will not listen to
the voice of the Lord,
if you rebel against the
commands of the Lord,
then the hand of the Lord
will strike you down!"

He who shouts in vain
from his paltry pulpit
like a decrepit Jesus
without followers.
He whose aging voice
is increasingly lost in
the traffic noise and
the hubbub of the crowd.

He who has become
a perennial fixture,
common as a lamppost
or a crack in the sidewalk,
ignored by the nefarious
creatures of the night
as they pass on their
way to nefarious deeds.

He who grows smaller
and smaller in God's
grand scheme of things,
until he is invisible
to all but himself.

ROSE AND THE WHITE STALKER
Boston-Manzetti

It's raining outside. Rose feels safe beneath the orange ceiling of the restaurant. Her soul is dry. Her senses savour *pâté de foie gras*, oysters, eggplant, the subtle bouquet of a Montrachet rising from a crystal goblet. She is at a sponsored company dinner with co-workers, not friends, few of them even acquaintances, none that will see her safely to the waiting haven of her car parked several blocks away. She watches their animated faces. She nods when they speak, though their conversation is an unintelligible buzz to her. She doesn't like to be out this late, but nothing matters as long as it keeps raining. Her nightmare will be caged in the deep furrows of her mind as long as it keeps raining. The rain is her shield. Just the sound of it can wash her mind clean. He will not come for her as long as it keeps raining.

The dinner is winding down. So is the rain. Rose is headed for her car, alone and lonely as usual. The rain feels good on her cheeks. She hurries down the street, the clack of her heels too loud on the concrete walk. The sound unnerves her as it echoes off darkened storefronts. She walks along the river, the shadows of the buildings like knives skim along her ankles. Splashes of darkness stain her coat and dress. A lizard darts across her path, its green tail wriggling into the hole of a basement. It smells a hunter on the prowl and its survival instinct is sharp.

Her car is a block away, she's almost there, but all at once the rain has deserted her. From the edge of a dark billboard, holding the tattered remains of some obliterated advert, a pallid face peers at her.

Him again! Her nightmare glowing in the belly of the dark like a burst of light from some canvas executed by a mad Caravaggio, a visage with a hunter brain inside that is tracking her.

She rushes past. But dark thoughts, their roots deep within, continue to haunt her, drawing a white skin that gives shape to a piece of darkness. The same hallucination in her dreams, in her thoughts, that only disappears with the rain. She inhabits the macabre theatre of a scene repeated endlessly, a Grand Guignol of weary madness.

Rose looks up at the dim heavens. She doesn't see any stars and takes that as a sign it will rain again. Then her white stalker will slip back into the funnel of whatever hell has granted him substance. She starts the engine of her Ford Escort, the only escort that ever accompanies her, and drives away from the river, away from a street with too many shadows, too many hungry mouths, too many billboards for her ghosts.

Rose suddenly brakes, avoiding at the last moment a body stretched in the middle of the road. A dark coat moves, a face slowly turns toward her, a colorless face with a foreboding smile. Her hands begin to tremble on the wheel, her foot on the brake. It's him. The stalker come to claim his prey.

He approaches and opens the door behind her and takes a passenger seat, even though she is sure she locked all the doors when she started the car. He is so impossible to deny it makes her want to scream. But Rose cannot scream. She can't do a single thing except grasp the wheel tightly as possible to still her trembling.

"Drive" he says, just like that book she always meant to read. Rose eases her foot off the brake and drives. She is afraid to look in the rear-view mirror, terrified she will see his smile leering back at her.

"Turn right."

Each time he speaks he leans close and she can hear his breath and feel its chill on the back of her neck. She turns as directed, hoping that if she does everything he tells her to do and offers no resistance, he might let her live once he is through with her. Assuming she would still want to live by then.

"Park," he says.

Running one tire up the curb and down, Rose manages to park the car at a slight angle to the curb.

She is no more than a marionette moving to the directions of a monosyllabic master. She has no clue as to where he has taken her, some section of the city she has never visited, or perhaps only visited in her worst nightmares. There are no streetlamps, no open bars or restaurants. It is a world of shadows overlapping shadows until the dark is so thick it seems a palpable weight. Her eyes search futilely for some point of reference.

"Keys," he demands, reaching one arm over the seat, palm up.

Rose turns off the ignition and drops the keys into his open palm, careful not to touch him. His hand is more than twice the size of hers. Before she knows it he is opening her door and yanking her from the car, one icy hand clamped to the nape of her neck. Once more she begins to tremble uncontrollably.

He pushes her forward. She senses more than sees walls rising up on each side of her. They are in a narrow causeway that quickly ends in a cul-de-sac. He shoves her against the end wall and forces her down onto the cold pavement.

"Stay!" he commands, as if she were no more than some animal he has trained. Then he turns and leaves.

Rose waits, crouched in the alley, counting off the minutes of life that remain to her, knowing he will soon return to claim his prey, knowing this is the fate she has always conjured for herself in her mind. But the minutes pass and he doesn't return. Instead the rain begins to fall once more. She realizes he has disappeared back into darkness, that he has finished with her for tonight.

She staggers back toward the street, brushing herself off as best she can. She finds the car where she parked it, her purse on the seat and keys lying beside it. Once behind the wheel it takes her several minutes before she is able to start and drive away, searching for a familiar street so she can find a route home.

This time was the farthest he had ever taken her, and Rose knows that next time could be all the way.

Watching the pendulum of the wipers on the rain-spotted glass, she silently prays for rain and more rain, a rain to end all rains, one that could wash her mind clean of the cold white darkness that infests it like a disease.

CANNIBAL AT LARGE
Manzetti

Harry, my mentor,
my companion and keeper,
always wears his blue coat
with seven bone buttons,
listens to Johnny Cash songs,
even in summer.

Harry loves music,
covering the noise of the slaughterhouse
and the rhythmic dance of his cleaver.
Harry loves white Burgundy,
which brings out the best
in his favorite delicacies.

He walks with the same, slow pace
as a survivor of the apocalypse,
while his gaze is fast,
because anything can become prey.

I'm his only friend,
except for Moon,
his green and orange-crested iguana.
Moon knows him as I do:
the earthquakes of his headaches,
the kicks of the forbidden impulses,
the fridge in the basement
housing his leftovers.

Moon is guarding its Master:
banishing Death from his bed,
banishing Life from his home,
a bride in a white dress
who would scour his kitchen,
remove the knives, clean up his mind.
The love of a reptile is strange
and intractable.

Every night Harry waits for me
over the river bridge, always the same,
to ask me the same questions:
"Eva, can I bite you?"
"Can I eat your breasts?"
I know desire is stronger than his will.
I know, every time, when I say no,
he will look for love elsewhere,
a kind of love to swallow,
unbearably delicious,
the dreams of a mad god.

Harry is my father.
Harry is my mother, too,
for she is inside him
in his blood,
for the last twenty years.

One day I will be quite small
to follow in her footsteps,
into the red hallways

that branch out from
the engine of his stomach.

EUGENE'S HURT
Manzetti

The hooker is sleeping,
the rain rocking her
with its bewitching rhythm,
scratching at the window.
Eugene lies by her side,
half-awake, drowning
in hypnagogic dreams
of his own creation.

He looks at the sky
that is growling and drooling.
He pulls up the collar of his coat,
feels the propellers of fear
churning in his thoughts
as he crosses a river of cars
where accursed souls are trapped
and reaches the other side.
The manhole, finally! Eugene thinks,
while it starts to rain.

He is going to turn into a rat,
a slimy swollen tail
pops out from his pants,
and his brain starts broadcasting
in black and white,
like the old TV of his mother,
the Fire Lady, long since

burnt with all in her building.

Eugene must take shelter immediately,
go down in the sewers,
into the cylinder of the dark,
cozy as a warm uterus,
He must put a thick cover
between him and the damned sky
that is pissing its nightmares
like primordial soup.

But maybe it's too late!
The rain has already hit him;
his skin burns and his second
heart is beginning to boil.
He can't tear it from his chest.
He must keep it inside,
between the cage of ribs.
His rat's muzzle rises,
his animal senses are straight
as the fur of drowned rats
stagnating under a green crust
in the waters of the river.

Eugene wakes up, wincing,
trembling like thousands
of blades of grass
below the rotating mouth
of a giant mower.
Like a trapped rat

he escapes with a leap
and hides himself under the bed.
From the three curtains of light,
the coverlet that surrounds him,
the hands of his mother stick out,
five, six, maybe seven:
they try to take him,
grabbing him by the tail.

The rain continues to fall
on the old yellow buildings,
over the sticky walls of the brothel.
The hooker turns on one side,
mumbling in her sleep
on a sky of goose feathers
above Eugene's small world:
two meters by three, same space
as the closet in his mother's house.
That smell of rotting orchids,
hairspray, the suffocating scent
of dirty perfumed lingerie,
and then the assault,
the nails of the Fire Lady
drawing on his flesh:
hunting scenes, barking, shouting.

The rat is trapped,
and above, from the cracks
of forlorn childhood,

near a nest of hornets,
the rain is dripping.
He feels it flowing over him,
around him, inside of him.
And it hurts.

REQUIEM IN A TAXI
Boston-Manzetti

China gets in the taxi.
The chorus of Mozart's *Requiem*
imprisoned by the stereo speakers
merges with her thoughts.
A hundred voices surround her,
vibrations touching her
thighs, heart, and breasts.

Between her fingers China tightens
the cold spheres of her necklace,
passing from one pearl to another.
With this heretic rosary
she counts her customers,
more than a hundred,
more than the singers of the choir.

The taxi driver stops
and turns up the volume.
The chorus of the *Requiem* now thunders:
Confutatis maledictis
Flammis acribus addictis.
China feels her legs burning.
A hell's manhole must have opened
under the rear seats of the taxi.

The driver turns to her,
his face like that of her father,

lord of whiskey and punches,
buried now three years
in a loose blue suit.

The driver is waiting for
her to get out of the cab.

China wants to abandon
these endless taxi rides,
the macabre rollercoaster
that Slade demands of her,
rides that rage her
mind with emotions
she must leave behind.

Legs still burning,
China stumbles onto the sidewalk.
Been to this address before.
Knows what will follow.

No need to pay the driver.
Slade takes care of that.
Just like everything.

THE XACTO KILLER: INTERIOR MONOLOGUE
Boston

So I fucked up the fourth one. Four by their count. No one's perfect.

The first two were nurses, nurses on the late shift. No challenge there. I watched them walk home several nights in a row, trailed them at a distance. Checked out the routes, the best places to hide. Then I struck. Out of a side street or alleyway, from the recessed doorway of a darkened storefront, out of the shadows like a nightmare they never expected in their abridged lives.

They didn't stand a chance. In one stroke, swift and clean, moving like a dancer, I passed the silver blade across their throats. Severing the carotid artery. It was beautiful! Each one fainted in seconds. Both the same way. Just clasped one hand against their throats and their heads rolled back and they fell, blood spilling across their collars and down their starched uniforms. Both were probably dead by the time they hit the pavement.

After the two nurses, they doubled the cop patrols round hospitals. But the urge was upon me again so I moved on to hookers. Not that Jack the Ripper is any hero of mine. In some ways a man after my own heart, but he never got credit for all he accomplished. When they take me down I'm going to get the credit. Every last bit of it and more.

The first whore was easy, already standing by the alleyway, like a target in a shooting gallery waiting to be nailed. Grabbed her by the waist, hauled her back a few feet and that was that. She turned toward me when she fell. The look of surprise and horror on her face was delicious. Better than in any film I've seen.

How was I to know the second slut was a tranny. With those long legs and full breasts, he/she looked like the real thing. Bitch grabbed my arm before I could cut her/him. Knocked the blade clean out of my hand.

I ran, what else could I do?

So they found the knife. No sweat there. I was wearing gloves. But now I got a name in the papers. The Xacto Killer. Wasn't even an Xacto Knife, just a cheap utility knife knock-off. Good enough to do the job. No need to sharpen it. You just switch blades when it gets dull. Good grip and cuts just deep enough for my needs.

Though I sort of like the name. It fits me now that I think about it. The exact precision of the ritual when it goes right.

Like I said, nobody's perfect. I know they will catch me eventually, but I'll have my day before they do. And when they do, I'll not only confess, I'll tell them about the other ones, before I came here. Maybe I'll even make some up.

Then I won't be anonymous or Xacto anymore. I'll be famous by my real name, not the one the tabloids have tagged me with. And they will know me by my real name and never forget it. Never! For the rest of their worthless goddamned lives!

DEEP IN HIS COMA
Boston-Manzetti

Jean-Paul dreams he is a moth,
his wings laced with intricate
curlicues and glyphs that conceal
the secret equations of gods,
the powder that velvet-dusts
his wings composed
of the finest grade cocaine.
Each time he flaps them
it fills the air he breathes,
taking him higher.

Dreams he is a thief
who can fly, dreams of
a thousand unlocked
doors and open windows,
from which he reaps
riches unimagined:
rare coins and stamps,
diamond bracelets
and emerald pendants,
masterpiece paintings
from the Renaissance
to the Impressionists,
even fine ladies waiting
in their canopied beds
to spread their legs.

Then his wings disappear
and his dreams change.
He is running along the
banks of that damn river
where Marinella was thrown,
the most beautiful woman
he had ever known
when his eyes were not
those of a thief.

Now the dreams are slipping
over the brim of his mind,
over rings of solid gold,
like the golden chain
on the image of the Virgin Mary
that hangs round his neck.

Beyond his pants stained with gunpowder,
the other thief, the real thief
who took her away on a spring day
with his black Mercedes,
black as the feathers of a crow
with two small red wings
printed on the long car doors,
the Pussycat's Coat of Arms,
his downtown strip club.

Jean Paul dreams again
the dust road, that door
where he went back

knocking a thousand times,
not knowing she was dead,
not ever realizing
that the river turned red
only to warn him.

But now he can see her again:
Marinella eyeless, with bruised lips,
her head sticking out of the waters
to look for the broad-faced bastard
that fired three times
and threw her in the river:
because there was no wine at home,
because her skin was ten-years-too-old
for his taste and the preference
of his best customers.

The wings of Jean-Paul bloom again,
piercing the skin of his back,
projecting him upward from
where he can see the entire city:
the hum of lights,
the failed neon of souls,
where he can perceive
the tail of his past,
stalled for years at traffic lights,
the head of the future
hissing from a manhole
with the language of a snake,

the open belly of the present
dripping seconds, minutes,
into cocaine white baggies
to be sold for a few dollars
to the first passing desperate.

From above, on the edge of space,
Jean-Paul can now see
the large irregular crater
of his crashed life,
and the watery grave of Marinella
that continues to flow
as a blue hallucination
around the Tropic of Cancer.

His consciousness expands
farther than space-time
should allow a man
of petty dreams.
He sheds emotion like
flesh slashed from bone.
He sees Sol shrinking,
it's system left behind.

He perceives the universe
in its elaborate complexity
and what it contains,
the cause and effect
of burning stars and people,
the push and pull

of inanimate matter
and animate across
an endless game board.

Then his eyelids begin to flutter
in the diminished light
of the prison hospital
where his body lies.

ROSE'S TRAUMA
Boston-Manzetti

The rain is black as the night. It splashes on the cyclops eye of the traffic light, emphasizing its red highlights, its blood without body fed by electric veins. The drops continue to fall, dripping to the skin of the Earth, beating a steady tattoo on the asphalt strip that divides the grass and the dark sunflower fields to the right and left. Rain teases the car, going round and around it, licking its tires, infiltrating into its smallest slits, as moisture in the coronary arteries of its engine. Rain looks through the car's fogged windows, draws crystal circles on them with its fingers, then clings to the car's canopy, resisting the wind, wailing a weak blues tunelessly, like a breathy harmonica without stops.

The wind and rain are crying for the child Rose, who feels safe and warm sleeping against the shoulder of her father as he clutches the steering wheel one-handed, tightening the curves, his free hand exploring Rose's small lean thighs. He smiles at the road ahead, showing all his yellow teeth. The rain senses his illicit caresses, it hardens and beats on the car's body with fists of ice. The hailstorm awakens Rose, the hailstorm averts the hand of her father from her virgin flesh, from her closed petals, from that garden of earthly delights, an aphrodisiac of blood roses that awaits him.

At last they are home, the rain falling more gently. Rose runs up the stairs to her room, she tightens the balls of her pearl necklace, too large and heavy for an eleven-year-old child. It's her talisman, the one around the neck of her mother when she saw her floating in the bathtub with her sunken blue eyes, while behind her, the smell of death ran away through an open window leaving a dense sweetish stench in its wake. On the dry point of her mother's gray, gnarled tongue, protruding from bloodless lips, her last words were still hanging. "You?"

Rose opens the windows and slips into bed, lulled by the music of the rain, by its glass harmonica that dispels the memories continuing to fill the bathtub with their dark mood: the blue eyes disappeared forever, the black plastic cloaking the silhouette of her mother, inflated at head and feet, moved by police; the rosary of words "Suicide... Suicide...Suicide" repeated endlessly by strangers who wear white coats; her father washing his hands and staring at his teeth in the mirror, while the house is emptied of music, while the stars, embedded in the cover of night, disappear, to be replaced by blue ambulance sirens and flashing lights.

It wasn't raining that night. That night was tasteless, the sky open and mute.

Rose fastens on the rain, letting it wash away everything, untying the knots and drowning the lizards that bite at her heart. Her bedroom window, loose in its old frame, suddenly slams shut. Rain leaves its breathy harmonica in the mud, sits in the garden behind an oak tree, chewing blades of grass, biding its time. Rose closes her eyes and dampens her breath.

A strange man enters her room, a phantom in white, a man with skin like snow, with a wedding ring on his finger. Rose thinks that this creature has married her dead mother, taking her to his home beneath some swamp, beneath waters covered in lilies with blue eyes, a few miles from the skyscrapers of the city that light the swamp's foamy crust with a dim phosphorescence that belies the decay within.

Rose closes her eyes and breathes under the sheets, trying to be quiet as possible, but that doesn't stop the man with white skin. He gasps as if her mother's lungs full of water dwelt in his chest. The fingers of the creature are long and insistent, they know how to find all the slits and crevices, how to spread the soft mesh of her body. "Let me in, sweetie." The man with flesh white and cold as snow steals the voice of her father and his pungent whiskey breath. "Let me in, sweetie, let me in!"

Rose thinks she is dreaming, that there can't be a tunnel, a passage long enough to connect the swamp and her bedroom, the world of the living and the world of the dead must remain separate. But when she opens her eyes the creature rears its back, its torso in shadow stretching like dark dunes, its sweaty head descending to rummage between her legs, between the petals of her field, which no longer reach toward the heavens but bend their stalks to the ground to scavenge the last drops of rain.

By morning rain as returned, nattering against the window, telling Rose to wake up. But Rose is no longer there.

She has retreated into a world that denies the reality around her. Listless, mute as an empty sky, she stares blindly at the floor or a bare patch of wall, immersed in visions that exist only in the cordoned-off chambers of her mind.

Her penitent father can't handle her, can barely stand to look at her. A man without a wife gets lonely, he tells himself, a man without a wife still has needs.

Rose is deposited with an aunt, an older sister of her dead mother. She is a frivolous and sickly woman who nevertheless manages to love and dote upon the withdrawn child, eventually coaxing her back to some semblance of normality. But the careless freedom and enthusiasm of childhood have fled. Rose's flesh has been harvested and will remain fallow.

EUGENE HATES THE RAIN
Boston

Hates the way it
raises the stink of city
from the thick air
and the damp pavements,
the garbage and ashes,
sweat and blood,
and carbon monoxide.

Hates the feel
of the rain,
how it plasters
the hair to his skull
and sends icy droplets
down the nape of his neck
to dampen his collar.

Hates the way
it shrouds windows
with its liquid scatter,
so he can no longer
see out of the world
in which he is trapped.

Hates the sound of the rain
like the static on a radio
when a station signs off,
and sometimes he can

hear voices in that static,
the cajoling voices
of doctors at the asylum,
the curses and accusations
of his dead mother,
voices of authority
and insanity stumbling
over one another
in an unintelligible rush.

Most of all
Eugene hates the way
rain can strangle fire
in its first breaths,
killing it in its bed
before it has a chance
to rise up and live
and breathe.

AWAKENING
Boston-Manzetti

Jean Paul is walking along the river.
He has left the stench of disinfected souls
trapped in the prison hospital
in a sea of starched white bed sheets,
where crucifixes and globefish
swollen with pissed memories float.

The river flows like a snake,
leaving past and present behind.
Jean Paul thinks that Marinella,
the siren with three bullets in her heart,
is pulling the strings of the current.
She wants to be remembered
in the dark pantheon of his limbo,
where nothing remains for long.
Not in this transformed life,
where even the air of the city
no longer smells or tastes the same.

A painter is bent over his canvas.
A necklace of bones protrudes from his shirt,
bumps on the vertebrae of his back.
Jean Paul stares at the unfinished canvas.
The river bridge is sketched midway
yet the painter never reaches the other side.
The man constantly deletes pieces
of the bridge as he paints them,

retreating to the middle to start over.
Like a rubber band taut beyond its limit,
snapping back to sting his palm.

Jean Paul understands the painter
is afraid to reach the other shore,
where the buildings are older,
where grotesque gargoyles
perched above the eaves
with wings about to spread
can dive on the heads of passersby,
stealing time and memories
of days yet to be lived.

The painter stops, moves a cigar
on the right of his mouth to the left.
He crosses his arms and gives up,
handing the brush to Jean Paul.
The sinuous river takes a pause,
anchored to the bottom by green stones.
ripples of motion-past spreading
in widening circles across its surface.
The head of Marinella slides over the water,
resembling a plastic float with no eyes.
Time disintegrates in the ripples
and no longer flows like a snake.

Jean Paul paints the missing pillars
and the cement pylons of the bridge,
the graceful arcs of its hanging cables,

until he reaches the other side.
The painter closes his eyes,
refusing to look at the future
that rises from the farther shore.

One night the painter
dreamed of a tomb
He felt the scent of dried flowers
and saw Death limping
between narrow alleys of marble
with many names and dates
and forgotten sentiments
carved on the right and left.
Kneeling slowly, his bones creaking
with some ghastly rhythm,
Death began to lick a headstone
as if it were a vanilla powder cake.
On it was engraved: 'Matt Baker,
February 15, 2001 - April 23...'
The painter woke suddenly,
thrashing among damp sheets,
still struggling free from
the tendrils of the dream,
listening to the incessant
rasp of his old lungs.

Jean Paul continues to paint the future
on the other side of the bridge,
discovering this new ability

born in the nest of his coma:
his drug dealer crushed by a truck,
colors splashed from all sides:
the shiny black of the big tires,
the silver of the dented grill,
the spatter of fresh blood,
which drips on the canvas
and onto the asphalt
at the same time.

Then, farther, under the scrawled
façade of an edgy gothic edifice,
Jean Paul draws a man with a cigar
kneeling on the steps of a white church
where all the colors in the sky are dripping.
The man seems to be praying
for those yellows, greens and blues
to flow all together, into another
world and a different creation.

The painter peeks at the canvas,
the scene of the colors, a rainbow
with a steering wheel and a driver
that may to be able to slip into
new streets and boulevards
that have yet to be named.
He's hoping for a transfusion
to fill the veins of his son, Matt,
who lives in a hospital room

next to a monster of steel
with ten eyes lit by LEDs
and lean arms of silicone.

The monster mixes cocktails
with the blood of the boy,
centrifuging young dreams,
platelets and cells always fresh.
Matt hopes to survive another day,
crossing the bridge once again,
dragging his ruptured kidneys,
grasping the veined yellow
and blue hands of his father.

Jean-Paul paints over the
future he has envisioned and
returns the brush to the painter,
who spits the butt of his cigar
into the grass and frowns
at the unfinished canvas.

Jean Paul continues his stroll
along the river parkway.
He sees men playing chess,
sitting on crude stone benches,
hunched over stone tablets
that rise like rigid mushrooms
from the damp and grassy earth.
He'd learned the game as a child
but abandoned it years ago.

Now he can't help laughing
as he watches the men play.
How ludicrous their moves are.
Just as his coma revealed
the push and pull of the cosmos,
he now perceives the lines
of force and intersection
and the endless possibilities
upon every field of play,
the future of every game.

Jean-Paul finds a man sitting alone,
still waiting for an opponent.
They play for a few dollars.
Sicilian Defense, Najdorf Variation.
Jean Paul doesn't know it.
by name, he just understands
the board and the pieces
and how they must move
to lead to checkmate.

He plays another man and
another until none of them
will play him anymore.
Jean-Paul leaves them sitting
around their stone mushrooms,
staring at one another in disbelief.
He leaves with a considerable
roll of cash in his pocket.

He has discovered a new
and far easier vocation.
No need to thieve anymore.

On the other side of the river
the falling sun wreathes the
buildings in a fierce corona,
and Jean-Paul can feel a great
heat rising from across the water.
He visions the city in flames
and knows he must leave
before it incinerates in the
furnace of its own corruption.

Far downriver where
the past recedes forever,
where deep currents churn
the dirt and debris of the delta
in whirlpools and eddies,
Marinella's bodiless head bobs
aimlessly in the muddied waters,
in line for a peaceful grave
beneath the tides of the sea.

LADY OF THE DARK HOURS
Boston-Manzetti

Nina and her beads of sweat
hypnotize herds of eyes
and nomadic souls,
dancing close to the
scattered web of tables
in a club that seems
to lie a thousand meters
beneath the edge of humanity,
between the writhing
coral tongues of its patrons,
lives stuck in reality and
heads hanging in a dream.

She is a lady of the dark hours,
the orange and blue rosette
hiding her cathedral where
flowers close their toothy petals,
swallowing dreams and mist.
Nina pushes buttons
on the bare backs of men
and between their legs,
switching them on and off;
vortices are tattooed round
her navel and the dark
mystery she withholds.
She swallows time and

the taut singularities
of time unraveled.

Feathers on her shoulders
are torn from the wings
of trapped men who grasp
and shake themselves while
the muscles of Nina swell
in sinuous motion.

She is a lady of the dark hours,
the peeled skin of the city,
coal turned to diamonds.
When her breasts rise
and fall with her breath,
drawing whistles and applause,
when her thighs rotate
and jump the silver pole,
when her ankle bracelets sing
and her toe rings glitter,
sensuous thoughts seem
to spring from her hair
like the snakes of Medusa
to bite watchers and dreamers.

She is a lady of the dark hours,
scythe and cold obsidian.
When you see in the distance
the black sails of the night raised
by scrawny ghosts of Myrmidon,

and Nereids in the open sea,
when you search for yourself
eyes closed, among the
branched streets of the city
with hands and heart sweaty,
with the fear of meeting
your addict doppelganger
on a bed of rotten leaves
in the company of madness,
Nina will dance on your belly
with a rib of tomorrow
held between her teeth.

BETRAYED BY THE RAIN
Boston-Manzetti

"You must like rain," the man behind the counter at the corner grocery says to her. "You only come shop in rain."

Rose glances up at him, but only for a second. She doesn't like to make eye contact with anyone. She knows his voice and accent by heart but she has never really looked at him before. He is wearing a turban and his unkempt beard looks prickly and is salted with gray.
Rose doesn't say anything. She doesn't trust foreigners and just wants to be left alone. She lays a twenty on the counter and waits for her change.

Outside the store she stops for a moment under the awning before opening her umbrella. She watches the silver droplets bouncing on the pavement, granting the world a liquid sheen, erasing the hard edges of things. She loved the sound of the rain on the awning, on the roof and windows of her three-story walkup, even on her umbrella when she walks in the rain. When she cannot sleep at night, she sits for hours by her window watching the rain come down. Sometimes the rain evokes strange and marvelous visions in her head.

The outlines of buildings bend to the ground, to drink from puddles with their concrete mouths. The red and white lights that pass on the road are freed from their plastic prisons to merge and fly apart in firefly dances of courtship and mating...the grass of flowerbeds stretches its muscles to weave new hedges, forming complex mazes with living corridors where the ghosts of children run, brandishing plastic swords and pulling the nylon cords of colorful kites...on the corner in front of The Starry Plough Tavern, a man with no legs has staked out his claim on a square of sidewalk. He is worshipping the rain, spreading his arms and letting it drench his palms. The lost faces of his wife and son bloom like fleshy petals from his palms. The rain is nourishing this homeless man, quenching his thirst for the past...

Rose could fall into a mindless trance watching the rain and the visions it engendered. Sometimes she would watch for too long, after the rain had stopped, and all at once her thoughts would be flooded with vile images until she tore her eyes away.

Troops of the men dressed in white, faceless, marching under her window like the vanguard of a macabre invasion...one phalanx of this ghoulish army drags the corpse of her mother with long steel cables and hooks attached to her body. She's dressed as a bride, her ivory train supported by a cadre of river rats. Her veil blows back, revealing her waterlogged features, her eyes like slits between her swollen cheeks and brow ...at the end of this procession, inside a jagged cage of white bones, her mother's disembodied heart pulses fiercely as if still making a claim upon life...and then Rose hears the white soldiers tramping up her stairs and chanting...

From the east there is a slender flash of lightning arcing

down from the clouds. A few seconds later a cannonade of thunder rolls through the street, echoing off the buildings that line it. Rose is startled out of her reverie. She opens her umbrella and shakes her head, dispelling the remembered images that haunt her. They retreat back into her unconscious but never vanish completely.

Rose strides into the rain, feeling safe, as she heads back to her apartment. A few doors from her building, as she is crossing an alleyway, an arm reaches out to encircle her waist, a hand reaches farther to cup one breast, pulls her back into the darkness. Rose drops the bag of groceries and her umbrella, but is too startled to scream. Then there is a sharp pain across her throat. She reaches up and her hand comes away covered with blood. The arm lets go of her and she collapses onto the pavement in shock. As she loses consciousness, her last thought is to wonder why the rain has betrayed her.

The rain continues to fall, caressing her face with its watery fingers, perhaps trying to wake her. But it's too late now, and at last at peace, she probably wouldn't want to wake up anyway.

OBSESSED WITH AUTUMN
Manzetti

I enter the orange light.
Autumn is waiting for me behind the door
with a diamond in her navel
and a pomegranate in her hand.
The light is floating, like a small lake
around her bare feet
and its canoes of blue polish.
A primordial puddle
reflects my oldest face,
my mask of Babylon
covered by the juice of the placenta
of my mother.

I close my eyes, as always
she goes down on my hips,
opens my womb, gently,
and looks inside. She stretches
her arm into my warmth,
searching for my dynamo, my engine;
she cuts the red and blue cables of my heart,
squeezing them between her fingers.

Lips covered with red seeds,
sing a primitive lullaby
on my skin, into my stomach,
echoing like the reassuring sounds
hummed by females adorned with jewels of bones

and purple stripes of resin around their eyes;
she devours me like a pomegranate
then places me on the bedside table
along with the others.

While Autumn sings
her fingers raise tides;
she fills me with honey and leaves of oleander,
with the cold grains of her sweat;
then she closes my belly,
sewing it with a thin silk thread,
but my dynamo, my hearth is out
there, dripping, in the third row
of her collection of pomegranates.

My time with Autumn is already over.
She disappears behind the door.
I go down in the yard, it's cold outside.
I walk fast, hoping not meet him again,
but he grabs me by the arm
"Hey, Romeo!"
The pimp, with a pomegranate tattoo on his neck,
spits on my coat: "See you next time."

He doesn't know that Autumn is the snow,
the cold skin of the mountain
smiling at its loneliness,
making thousands of footprints
disappear in moments,
He doesn't know that

I will cut his throat,
the next time
I go back to the peak.

SANDOVAL BITTERS: INTERIOR MONOLOGUE
Boston

Goddamned private DNA Lab! I could have been a hero if not for them. I could have nabbed the Xacto Killer. How much of a hero can you be for catching a fucking dead man?

There were no fingerprints on that knife the son-of-a-bitch dropped, but it was old. There was dirt in the groves of its handle. It had been used for other things besides slicing up women. So there could have been DNA on it. I was the one who was smart enough to send it in to be tested.

City this size should have its own fucking DNA lab rather than farming it out to some private concern. I bet the half-assed scientist bastards who work there make more money than I do. But do they run my sample marked "Urgent?" Does telling them we have a serial killer on the loose do any good?.

Three-and-a-half weeks!

I expected them to move like the wind, and instead I get a snail on valium

I checked out info on DNA samples. Should take less than 48 hours to process one. But the assholes at the lab say they are swamped with samples, backed-up. Yeah, backed-up testing for some shyster lawyers who pay them more than the city dies. Backed up trying to get some nigger out of slam for a crime he supposedly never committed. Though he probably belongs there for something else he did that was just as bad or worse.

Three-and-a-half fucking weeks!

The perverted bastard kills two more women in the meantime! We tell them to stay off the street alone late at night, to stay away from alleyways, but they won't listen. First, a Filipino woman who was working late closing up her dry cleaning store and headed for the subway. Then, a Rose something-or-other, secretary at a company that makes aluminum extrusions. Whatever the hell those are! She had been to the corner store and was on the way back to her apartment. We found the bag of groceries she dropped on the sidewalk at the foot of the alley and her body not far beyond. Both women dead in one stroke. Just like all of them.

The Filipino was fifty-three and overweight, the other thirty-something and dowdy as a haystack. Bastard didn't seem to care what they looked like long as they were women. From what the coroner said, neither of them put up a fight.

After the fifth killing, pressure was building on me, both in the department and the newspapers. Captain was on my back and making noises about putting someone else on the case. As if the everyday shit that goes down around here at night wasn't enough pressure on me already.

So the DNA results *finally* come back and there's a 93% match with a perp we've got on record. Joshua M. Markov, aka Mantis, a petty drug dealer who worked in a parking lot off Fifth and used it as a cover. Busted once for possession, not dealing, back in July. First offense so he got off with probation.

I was sailing high for about an hour. Lit up like a frigging Christmas tree, imagining the press conference I would hold and thinking maybe a promotion could be in the offing. Get my turn at the wheel. Get off this damned night shift!

Then we track him down. Turns out the creep got himself hit and killed by a truck last week. Dashed into the street right in front of it. That's what the driver said and witnesses confirmed it. Someone he cheated on a deal was probably chasing the scum down, that's the way I figure it. But it doesn't make a goddamned bit of difference how you cut it. The son-of-a-bitch was dead!

By now that sick puppy is dancing with the Devil, just where he belongs. But where the hell does that leave me? God couldn't even wait for me to track him down.

You just don't get much credit for catching a dead man. I hate this goddamned night shift.

DEATH METAL IN A TAXI/
STRAWBERRY FIELDS IN A CAR
Boston

China gets in the taxi.
Some Death Metal cut booms
from the stereo speakers.
She asks the driver to turn it down,
and he does, but the bass line
still reverberates monotonously
throughout the frame of the cab,
creeping beneath her flesh
and jarring her bones.

She watches the night streets
sliding pass in shades of shadow,
Except for the traffic lights and
their distorted reflections on
pavement still damp from rain,
the world is bleached of color.
The bass thuds on without respite,
making her teeth and gums ache.

The taxi climbs half a hill
and then eases in to the curb
on a block of tall dark houses
surviving from a different era.

China has to bend forward
to see the high gothic steeple

atop the house of her destination,
like something straight out of Poe.
She has been here twice before,
the second worse than the first.

She recalls the cadaverous man
with nicotine-stained fingernails,
his bloodless toothy smiles and
the eczema on his cheeks and
shoulders like the map of some
strange and horrible land she
would soon be forced to inhabit.
A shudder passes through her
slight frame from deep within.

Though he never harmed her
or threatened her in any way,
though he barely spoke at all,
China was convinced from one
look at his jaundiced eyes
that he wanted to kill her.

The driver has turned to her,
his face in shadow except for
a single gold tooth that catches
a strand of light from the street.
He is waiting for her to leave,
to accept her assignation and
whatever it might entail.

"Take me back," China says.
The driver shakes his head,
the gold tooth flashing dimly,
like a warning beacon on a
lost highway being excavated
by a road crew of the damned.

"Slade says you go," he tells her.
"I wait one hour, little more,
then take you back to him."

All souls, even the most
desperate and decadent,
have a line they cannot cross,
a time they had not reckoned
on until the moment arrives.

China gets out of the cab,
turns away from the house,
and heads back down the hill,
head bent and lips compressed.
She jaywalks at the intersection,
turns and sticks out her thumb.
She knows it won't take long.

The third car stops, a blue
coupe with a dented fender,
and the window slides down.
"I'm not hooking," China says,
aware of how she is dressed,

short leather skirt, stiletto heels.
"I just need a ride somewhere."

"No problem" the driver says,
"Where are you headed?"
He is young, early thirties,
clean cut, which doesn't
tell her much, but for some
reason she is not afraid.

China gets in the car and
hesitates before answering.
She thinks of Slade, the back
of his hand across her temple
the last time she disobeyed him.
her earache for days afterward.
And rumors of the penknife
he uses on the backs of those
girls who disobey too often.
"Where are you headed?"
she asks the driver in return.

"South," the man tells her,
"all the way to Middleton.
There's a chess tournament
with some tidy prize money."

China laughs. "So you make
your living hustling chess?
That's a new one on me."

"You and me both," the man
tells her. "You and me both."

"Middleton sounds good,"
China says, "Let's go."

Before he stopped for her,
before he even saw her,
Jean-Paul had already painted
their shared future in his head.
He likes its textures and colors
more than anything he has
envisioned for a long time.

China leans back and watches
the car consume the highway.
One of her favorite Beatle's
songs is playing on the radio.
The road is like an open door,
she thinks, to another world,
to anywhere away from Slade.
She takes a deep breath and
exhales, her first free breath
in more than two years.

THE GREAT UNKNOWN
Boston-Manzetti

i

Night, the Great Unknown,
rolled up in its own shadows,
waits with open jaws
for the night shift, the smell
of Detective Samuel Sandoval.
Night misses his old blue coat
from when he walked a beat.
It remembers the brass buttons
and the stale crumbs
of communion wafers
embedded in its threads.

Sandoval moves along
the riverside drive
followed by a skinny rat.
After an ten-hour shift,
he walks aimlessly
in the dark morning,
still high on adrenaline
and nicotine and hate.
He has to come down
before he can return
to his wife and children
and suburban refuge.

Sandoval hasn't been
to church for years.
He no longer remembers
the face of Jesus Christ.
The last time he saw it,
it was swinging on
the silver medallion
of an ethnic gang leader,
crudely carved with
no look of suffering
anointing its features.
Rather it smiled at him.
And so did the gang leader.
A mocking sarcastic smile
that seemed to be saying,
'Calvary, up to you now, man!'

Sandoval has been working
the night shift for five years.
He tries not to remember
the blood-scattered lines
and faults of that passage,
the lives lost along the way.
Night, the Great Unknown,
fate in bone-cold vestments,
is preparing his own demise,
dramatic and startling
or chill and indifferent
as the stone city itself.

ii

Rashida is sixteen-years-old.
Her boyfriend made her
swallow too many jelly shots.
Then he slapped her
because she would not
sleep with him,
because she wanted
to remain a virgin
until she was married.
For her, Sex is the
great dark Unknown.

She runs down the alleyway
to the riverside drive,
running away from
her boyfriend and herself,
running from a future
that is rushing too fast,
her teeth so very white
in the intermittent lights
spaced along the river.
In the long patches
of shadow in between,
Night, the Great Unknown,
claims her with its wing.

iii

Sandoval sees a flash to his right
moving fast, far too fast,
moving toward him,
a shifting flash and a shadow.
He imagines the blade of a knife
that shines in the river lights,
in the black leather of nowhere,
a blade that seeks his flesh.

"Not yet," he thinks "Not yet,"
while Rashida runs closer,
mouth open, breathing heavily.
Sandoval hears that harsh breath.
Night, the Great Unknown
touches the back of his coat
with its unsheathed claws.

"Chills. Do you feel them, man?"
"Yeah!"

In an extended fraction
of a fractured second,
Sandoval draws his
revolver from its
shoulder strap
and shoots blindly
— once! twice! —
aiming at that sharply

shimmering light that
is nearly upon him.
The shots echo off
the condominiums
that rise along the river.

"Calvary, up to you now, man!"
"'Who's speaking?" Sandoval asks.

The only answer is the
rush of the river passing.
The body on the ground
has stopped moving.

iv

Sandoval kneels beside
the body of Rashida,
curled on its side,
a silver lipstick tube
clutched in one hand.
She's no longer masked
by the wing of night.
Her face has become
that of a girl surprised
by a sudden rainfall,
by the first and last
thunder of her life.

"Your blood...is mine...,"

Sandoval whispers
to the dead girl,
to the Great Unknown.
He has never seen the
face of an angel before.

Twin windows light up
in the building that
rises above him,
throwing his shadow
on the cracked asphalt,
then a third window,
where the Great Unknown
suddenly appears
in its shadow flesh,
dressed as a tall magician
with a top hat on his head.

A snap of the fingers
lights his long cigarette.
He inhales deeply as
he savors the scene below
as if it were a work of art.
Then he exhales and
blows a coat of fog
across the city.

Sandoval hears a siren.
Someone has called
in the disturbance.

He knows he should run,
yet he remains standing,
half bent over the body.
Though his face is
in complete darkness,
its silhouette is composed
of hard angles and lines.

He realizes that
he won't be going
home to his family
and the suburbs tonight.
Instead he has been
crucified on the cross
of the Great Unknown.
Soon his own cohorts
will be coming with
their flashing lights
to carry him away.

"Calvary, man!"

I AM THE FIRE
Manzetti

Eugene "Two Hearts"
stares at the palace of the Eldorado.
A hooker, with her flamingo legs,
which could break any moment,
is about to enter the hall of the brothel
through an anonymous door on the right,
after passing the Bistro and two waiters
who are taking a break in front of it,
smoking cigarettes, counting their tips,
launching, with phantom slingshots,
their dreams into the foam of the river,
dirty with the debris of the slum,
where they will return late tonight
after having served steaks and faux smiles
to fat customers with Golconda diamonds
sparkling on their wrists and fingers,
and to vultures dressed as men
who dip their beaks in turtle broth.

The hooker is about to begin her shift.
She hastens for the last few meters.
The wind coming from the southwest
is blowing stronger and stronger
with its mouth wide as her loneliness.
Running on the asphalt with
a fur clasped around thin shoulders,
letting her silver hoop earrings swing,

the digital readout on the taximeter
attached to her belly whirling swiftly
like the symbols on a slot machine.

Eugene takes out of his pocket, gently,
his holy card of St. Joan of Arc,
kisses it, as he always does
when the fire is about to awaken.
Then he opens the trunk of his car,
takes two cans of gasoline,
and walks towards the brothel.
He is following the steps of his
mother's ghost, who burns
like a torch, while the night
obscures his vision with
the help of dead streetlights.

He breaks a window on the ground floor
of the Eldorado's palace, which is dozing
and dripping sperm from its beams.
After pouring the gasoline inside,
he lights the fire and savors
its sudden roar of vengeance,
 a tiger rife with repressed rage
who finds a sleeping human
confined in its circus cage.

Eugene mounts the front steps
of the brothel, covered by gasoline,
and rings the large brass bell.

Madame Desroches opens the door
and before she can say, as usual,
"Show me your money!"
Eugene lights himself on fire,
opens his arms, a burning living cross.

Then he embraces the old *maîtresse*,
warming her frozen heart
after so many mercenary years.

CONFLAGRATION
Boston-Manzetti

The fire is first reported on Saturday evening at 7:15 pm.
An old wood-frame building on the southern border,
where the river curls around the city before flowing north
to the sea, is in flames. The skies are clear of rain or clouds
and an uncommonly warm wind from the southwest is
fanning the blaze. It hasn't rained for over a week. At this
point only a one-alarm fire, but that would soon change.

* * *

Fire is devouring the Eldorado.
Eugene, his body in flames,
still manages to climb the stairs
and jump from a third-floor window.
He looks like a human comet
flying through a dark slice of night
before crashing onto a parked taxi.

The dyed hair of Madame Desroches
is burning, just like her old face.
She screams and beats at it fiercely,
while hookers and their fat customers
are running along the red velvet hallways
through the burning guts of the Eldorado,
searching for any escape from the flames.
They are all half-naked and frightened.
The Eldorado seethes like an inferno.

Yet there remains one who won't leave:
Lilla, a slim fifteen-year-old hooker
whose teeth are still good,
who was born in the Eldorado
and has never left it in her short life.
So far the fire seems not to want her,
perhaps because she doesn't yet
have enough memories to burn.

The Eldorado vomits naked bodies
from its red and flaming windows,
those who have fed it for years
now being expelled into the night.

* * *

Percussion Duelling Pistol, c. 1845,
American, barrel of Damascus steel,
breech and muzzle decorated with
inlaid gold, floral design on stock

Sandoval is home alone in his spacious
suburban refuge, cleaning and polishing
his gun collection, sipping blended scotch.
The television is on with the volume off.

Colt Rimfire Pocket Revolver,
nickel plated, .30 caliber, 1875,
snub barrel, rosewood grips

He is out on bail for a murder charge
in which he's the odds-on favorite

for a swift conviction followed
by years in a white-collar prison.

Colt Single Action Army Revolver,
.45 caliber, 1903, engraved by
Cumo Helfricht, patterned grip

A small collection, but pricey.
He has shells for each weapon
in a drawer beneath the case
where the guns are displayed.

Pair of German Target Pistols,
single shot, 1923, Otto Seelig,
engraved, checkered wood grip

His wife has left him with a note
and taken both children with her.
Never popular in the department,
he has no friends to talk with.

Colt Detective Special Blue,
1966, rearing colt engraved
above walnut-checkered
grip with silver medallion

Sandoval see a news bulletin
scrawling across the television.
Learning of the growing fire,
he thinks: Burn, baby, burn!

* * *

With the southwest wind growing stronger as the evening progresses, the fire cannot be contained. By 9:00 pm not only has it spread to warehouses along the banks of the river, but infested rows of houses and shopping and entertainment districts in the nearby slum. Engines from firehouses all across the city are dispatched to combat the blaze. Now it is a three-alarm fire.

* * *

"Come on, Sugar Baby, come on."

"We're not taking the fucking snake!"

Slade and Mary Ann are standing on the sidewalk outside the brownstone. He has already fled his own apartment, which by now is probably in flames. The fire is still blocks away, but the air is already full with streamers of smoke rising in the wind from the southwest. They can see sparks flying in the sky, pieces of flaming debris thrown from the updrafts of burning buildings.

"Come on, Sugar Baby, come on. Look, Slade! She's coming!"

The python has appeared at the top of the front stairs of the decrepit building and is slithering down toward the street.

"I'll buy you another snake! Now shut up and get in the damned car or I'll leave you behind, too!"

Slade throws Mary Ann's hastily packed suitcase into the trunk on top of his own and shoves the lid down. He grabs her by the wrist and ignoring her protests hauls her around to the passenger side of the Mercedes. Opening the door and throwing her roughly inside, he slams it after her.

"And stay there!" he shouts, leaning close to the window and raising a rigid forefinger.

Slade climbs in behind the wheel, turns the key, and peels away from the curb. Time to get out of this goddamned city, he thinks, where it always rains except when you need it. Mary Ann is rubbing her wrist and tears are running down her cheeks.

Left to her own, the python wanders into the street and slips down the dark shelter of a convenient storm drain to avoid the increasingly smoky air.

* * *

A lady of the dark hours
is standing at the seventh floor
window of her condominium
with a pair of binoculars
pressed tightly against her eyes,
so that when she removes

them they leave red circles
on the map of her flesh.

She is watching the fire spread.
She can't pick out the club where
she dances, where she is due
in less than hour for her first show
of the evening, but she can see
that entire section of the city
is already swathed in flames.

She is paid well fives nights a week
to be an untouchable icon of desire
for men addicted to her charms,
a symbol of absolute adoration.

She wonders how she will survive
without that salary, wonders how
much will she miss the worship?

Her body is in shape from dancing.
On stage, with the right makeup
and lighting, she can pass for
ten years younger than her age.
Off stage, in unmerciful daylight,
under the glare of overhead lights,
the ravages of a life lived too fast
for too many years are revealed.

She needs a man to take care of her,

an older man, stable and wealthy,
not too demanding or unattractive.
The same thing she has been
seeking for nearly a decade.

She turns away from the window,
fishes the ounce baggy out of the
top drawer of her nightstand,
and prepares another line
to ease her body and mind.

* * *

*Multi-alarm fire. The governor has declared a state emer-
gency and fire trucks from other counties across the state
are dispatched to combat the growing conflagration..*

*Soon refugees, with what possessions they can salvage,
some with loaded shopping carts as if they were homeless, which they suddenly have become, are fleeing from
their lost domiciles and north to City Center.*

*Unless the wind changes direction, it appears the western
part of the city will be spared: Spanish Town, The Chinese
Enclave, Little Italy, bohemian village.*

* * *

Slade takes a western route out of the city, away from the
fire. Then swings south, bypassing 66 to the west. Then
back east below the burning city. He can see the flames
across the river in the distance covering most of the

Southside, lighting up the sky. Then he turns his back on it and heads south along the Coast Highway, the route to warmer climes.

After each turn, the plastic Virgin Mary hanging from his rearview mirror swings back and forth, a memento from his early youth. He thinks of it as a talisman, the only superstition he has not left behind.

Escaping the city feels good, Slade is thinking. Lie on some warm beaches. Soak up the sun. Get started all over again. It wouldn't be hard. He could always find new girls. He liked doing it. And he had enough saved to carry him awhile.

"Get something on the radio," he tells Mary Ann. "Some jazz, not that rap shit you listen to."

She is sitting away from him against the passenger door, her body drawn in on itself. She is still rubbing her wrist even though it doesn't hurt.

"Get it yourself!"

Slade takes one hand off the wheel and punches her in the upper arm. Hard.

* * *

Camilla knows about the fire,
but it means nothing to her.
There is no fire in Spanish Town.

110

She sits at her favorite table
in the bar of the *Gracias Madre,*
from where she can see both
the room and the street.

She feeds the old jukebox
to listen to songs she has
heard many times before.
She carefully sips Bushmills
to help her on her way.
Sometimes she dreams of Diego.

Then she sees Gasoline,
standing outside the window,
wearing an old trench coat.

The mask of his face
is set in stone,
and his dark uncut hair
blows wildly in the wind.

* * *

*Soon after the first wave of refugees flows into the streets
surrounding City Center, the more dissident among the
crowd begin looting. There had already been protests for
over a week about the killing of a young black girl by a police detective. There is more destruction than theft. It is
the boiling over of a rage that has been repressed for too
many years on a day to day basis.*

Most stores have hurriedly closed. The ones that haven't, soon regret it. Displays are ripped apart, merchandise tossed asunder. Baseball bats are seized from a sporting goods department and the mob moves back into the street to break the windows of parked cars. Guns are discharged into the air, more than one bullet falling back to earth to strike a bystander. Squadrons of police in riot gear arrive to quell the violence and contain the crowds. Tear gas is released. Arrests are made. There are casualties and injuries on both sides.

* * *

Like so many others,
Harry, the gourmet cannibal,
has abandoned his home
and is fleeing north on foot
through the crowded streets.
headed toward City Center.

With an old brown suitcase
in one hand and cradling
his pet iguana Moon
under his free arm,
its leash trailing behind,
he hurries to keep pace
with the growing multitude
that surrounds him.

The crowds have spilled
onto the streets and

traffic is often blocked.
Moon maintains his
phlegmatic reptilian calm
through all of it.

Harry is worrying about
the choice tidbits lodged
in his basement fridge,
wondering if they will
survive the conflagration
and still be edible.

He is thinking about
his daughter and
her still-unsavored flesh,
hoping she will survive.

He is not used to walking
this far and this fast.
His breath is labored
and he feels lightheaded.

And Moon, normally
so well-behaved,
is suddenly squirming
under his arm.

* * *

Coast Highway. One hundred and fifty miles south of the
city. Well past Middleton. Getz and Gilberto mellow on

the car radio. Slade is enjoying opening the Mercedes up on the highway when a fog begins to roll in off the ocean.

"Slow down," Mary Ann tells him.

Slade has already slowed to sixty. He takes one hand off the wheel, reaches over, and punches her in the arm.

"But the fog!" Mary Ann wails.

If the fog hadn't rolled in so swiftly, if Slade hadn't turned to give Mary Ann one of his looks, that look none of his girls ever wanted to see twice, he might have swerved or braked in time. As it was, the rear of the slow-moving semi appeared out of the mist like a perfect engine of death.

It's bed was just the right height to rip the top of the passenger compartment off the Mercedes and decapitate both its occupants.

* * *

Nearly a fifth of the city is in flames or smoking ruins. The fire has reached Riverside Park. The trees and grasses are burning, threatening to spread the devastation to the condominiums farther north. The humid night air is filled with the constant wail of fire engines, ambulances, police sirens, burglar alarms, their solos and choruses howling like bloodhounds up from some vicious netherworld .

* * *

Fifteen hours into his shift with
no end in sight, Dr. Narayan
can no longer distinguish
the cries of human pain from
the sirens of arriving ambulances.
He is trapped by walls of sound
assailing his ears like hail.
Schools of dark tadpoles float
before his eyes, racing back
and forth across his vision.
The emergency room seems to
sink into the mouth of the Earth,
searching the underground
for its own place in Hell.

Dr. Narayan runs between
the stretchers that continue
to fill the crowded rooms.
All those faces, dead and alive,
are staring at him, whispering:
"Find your wife, you fool!"
They lick their torn lips
as if they are savouring
the taste of human flesh.

He lifts dozens of white sheets.
Some faces are unrecognizable,
covered with ash and blisters.
A priest with a scorched Bible

and a ruby on his ring finger
motions Narayan to stop.
The priest stands by the bed
of a woman contorted in pain,
body frozen in a final rictus,
one arm raised to her face
like a victim from Pompeii.

Touching the discolored
forehead of the woman,
the priest mumbles some
unintelligible benediction
from under his breath.
A butterfly with red wings
emerges from her mouth
and flies through the room.
Dr. Narayan looks away
from the dead remains
of what was once his wife.

He observes the jerky flight
of the butterfly that seems
to reproduce itself quickly.
With his eyes watered
by loss and madness,
he sees hundreds of them,
red sparks flying in the air,
devouring oxygen, shouting heat.
The great fire of the city has
reached the emergency room.

Sandoval is watching live coverage
of the conflagration on Channel 5.
Aerial views from traffic copters
reveal entire blocks in flames.
Multi-storied tenement buildings
that should have been demolished
years ago collapse in on themselves.
Gas lines explode like cluster bombs,
spewing the debris of abandoned lives.

Sandoval is for the most part oblivious,
trapped within his own dark thoughts,
searching for a solution to his dilemma.
Like a cold-case murder no detective
can unravel, there is no easy answer.

He considers fleeing to another state,
imagines his life as a fugitive on the run.
He envisions adventures along the way,
sees himself saving the life of a small boy,
exposing some corrupt union organizer,
having an affair with a mysterious woman
on a tramp steamer to South America.

Romantic nonsense derived from movies,
nothing to do with the reality he knows
he must face if he were truly on the run.
It would be a hand-to-mouth existence and

he would break more laws just to survive.
Sooner or later he would be apprehended.

Sandoval thinks of himself in prison,
incarcerated with white-collar swindlers
and embezzlers and crooked politicians,
no better than the blue collar ones he
has spent so much of his life arresting.
Some true sociopaths and far worse.
He would have nothing in common with
any of them, and they would look down
on him for the crime he'd committed.

And when he was finally released,
what would there be for him then?
Life as a security guard or watchman,
shunned by his wife and children,
concealing the shame of his past,
slowly drinking himself into oblivion.

Once again he sees the girl's body,
curled lifeless on the asphalt,
growing cold as the passing river,
the blood pooling from her side.
He relives the instants of his crime,
the rush of fears and frustration
that toppled him over the edge
of sanity and made him a killer.
That was not Samuel Sandoval
who fired those shots but some

vile creature bred for tragedy.
He prays to erase those images,
to forget those fractured instants.

There remains one hard answer
that would solve all his problems
and cover the wages of justice,
one he returns to over and again.
Sandoval views his prized collection,
small but pricey, wondering which gun
he would choose for that final sin.

* * *

The Weather Bureau had been predicting it since the day before. Not long after midnight a storm front hanging off the coast for the last two days came ashore hard, drenching the city in a heavy rainfall accompanied by high east winds. The wind and rain were soon laden with ash. Parts of the city that escaped the burning now received a share of its debris, staining buildings, streets, and cars.

With thunder sounding and lightning flashing in the sky, the crowds soon abandoned their violence. Most of the refugees were ferried by police vans or directed by police squadrons to shelters that had been hurriedly set up in school gymnasiums, auditoriums, and the recently defunct hockey rink.

Patches of the blaze still burned fitfully for several hours after the rain began to fall. Yet by morning nature had accomplished what man could not. The fire was over.

Yet for that day and the days following, you could still smell the damp ashen stench left by the burning and the rain throughout the entire city. There are some who believe that when the wind is right, you can smell it to this day.

LEGEND OF THE ALBINO PYTHONS
AND THE BLOODY CHILD
Boston–Manzetti

Slithering through the dark
bowels of the city in storm drains
where sewers often overflow,
the parthenogenic progeny
of an escaped pet python
survive on rats, unwary
city workers, and the odd
miscreant fleeing the law,
crushing the last breaths
from their trapped bodies.
Nightmares beyond reason,
they inhabit and haunt
these dank concrete
and steel corridors.

Some claim that through
generations born and surviving
in the fetid dark, they have
bred to albino pythons
capable of mesmerizing
their prey with a glance
of their lustrous purblind eyes.

Others say there will come
a day when they will emerge
from the rancid depths below,
from storm drains and manholes

and along the banks of the river.
Shunning the harsh light of day
they'll come in dead of night,
pale specters from hellish depths
devouring sinners in their beds.

Then there are those who
tell the story of a little girl,
seen after midnight, walking
barefoot through the dark
asphalt streets of the city,
wearing torn yellow pajamas
splattered with blood and
a pale young python twined
around her neck, a living,
breathing ophidian necklace.
She is the ghost of the city's
corruption made manifest,
a perverse little demon
with sharp young teeth.

They say it's her, with her
flaming hair, who leaves
a phosphorescent red trail
behind her, who was the
first to be dropped into
the sewers, the first to
have seen a nest of pythons,
to heat it with her human cells.

In revenge against those who
left her to a watery grave,
she has given to the snakes
an advanced intelligence,
a key to the weaknesses
of the Lords of the Earth
who walk on two legs.

If you meet her when
you're alone after midnight
and your own path turns
a phosphorescent red,
grasp a silver crucifix,
pray to your failed gods
for salvation, take off
your shoes and run away.

They call her Anja The Red,
this ghostly witness who
warns that in the underworld,
where your worst fears
and obsessions fester,
a reptilian dominion thrives,
waiting to embrace you
with its slick relentless coils.

Bruce Boston is the author of more than fifty books and chapbooks, including the dystopian science fiction novel *The Guardener's Tale*. His poems and stories have appeared in hundreds of publications. His poetry has received the Bram Stoker Award, the *Asimov's* Readers Award, and the Rhysling and Grandmaster Awards of the SFPA. His fiction has received a Pushcart Prize, and twice been a finalist for the Bram Stoker Award.

www.bruceboston.com

Alessandro Manzetti is the author of more than twenty books in English and Italian, including works of fiction, poetry, and nonfiction. His poems and stories have appeared in numerous publications. His poetry collection *Eden Underground* has won the Bram Stoker Award 2015, and his poetry collection *Venus Intervention* was nominated for the Bram Stoker Award 2014.

www.battiago.com

Ben Baldwin is a freelance artist and illustrator. He has produced book cover designs and magazine illustrations for publishers around the world, such as PS Publishing, Crystal Lake Publishing, TTA Press and Centipede Press. He has been short-listed several times for the British Fantasy Award for Best Artist.

www.benbaldwin.co.uk

] FUORI [
[COLLANA]

Kipple
officina libraria

Kipple Officina Libraria
Via Ignazio Canale 5/2
16029 Torriglia (GE) ITALY
www.kipple.it